Powwow

by Linda Coombs

Illustrated by
Carson Waterman

MULTICULTURAL CELEBRATIONS

MODERN CURRICULUM PRESS

Multicultural Celebrations was created under the auspices of The Children's Museum, Boston. Leslie Swartz, Director of Teacher Services, organized and directed this project with funding from The Hitachi Foundation.

Design: Gary Fujiwara
Photographs: 5, Carolyn A. McKeone; 6, Cornelia Hasenfuss; 21, Toni Weeden.

MODERN CURRICULUM PRESS, INC.
13900 Prospect Road
Cleveland, Ohio 44136

ISBN 0-8136-2267-0 (soft cover)   0-8136-2268-9 (Reinforced Binding)

7 8 9 10   95 94

Simon & Schuster   A Paramount Communications Company

It was the first morning of the biggest *Powwow* of the
summer. "M-m-m-m," Tina Howowswee thought as
she awoke to the smell of coffee and bacon cooking.
Feeling the crisp, cool morning air, she snuggled into
her sleeping bag for one last minute.

"T-i-n-a, there's hot water in the basin," she heard her father call from outside the tent. "Hurry and wash up before the boys get out here."

She poked her head out of the tent, squinting in the bright early sunshine. After washing and eating breakfast, Tina said, "I'm going to find Joanie. I'll be back before *Grand Entry* to get dressed."

She hurried past the other campsites and vendors' stands. Joanie and her family were *Penobscot* people from Maine. They made moccasins and ash splint baskets. Tina's family, the Howowswees, were *Wampanoags* from Massachusetts. They traveled all over from one *Powwow* to another during the summer. It was the only time the girls got to see each other.

2

"Tina! Over here!" shouted Joanie from her parent's stand. "I was hoping you would get here early. We still have time to walk around and see who's here."

"I'm so nervous today," Tina said. "This will be my first time competing."

"You? You shouldn't be nervous," Joanie said. "You are a good fancy dancer. You remembered all those steps Laurene taught us," her friend said. "And besides, everyone in your whole family is a great dancer."

Handmolded From
Nature\ colored Clay
of The
Gay Head Cliffs
By (Wild Cranberry)

"Well, I do have a new *regalia.* The only thing is my moccasins are getting too small."

"Look—there's Mary Wolf Runner. They came all the way from South Dakota. This *Powwow* draws so many people from other parts of the country."

The girls wandered from booth to booth, admiring the beautiful crafts for sale. There were ash and birch bark baskets from Maine and Canada, turquoise jewelry from the Southwest, and beautiful woven sashes and bags from Central and South American tribes.

6

Louis, Tina's older brother, appeared out of the growing crowd. "Where have you guys been? Mom was worried," he said. "She . . . "

"Good morning everyone," interrupted the *emcee* over the loudspeaker. "Welcome to the 6th Annual *Powwow*. Attention all dancers—please remember—*Grand Entry* will begin at 12:00 sharp!"

"Come on," Louis said. "I'll treat you to Navajo tacos before we get dressed. Or would you rather have buffalo burgers?"

"Oh, I couldn't eat a thing," Tina answered. "I'll just go back and get into my *regalia.*"

"Okay," Joanie said. "I'll see you at *Grand Entry.*"

Tina's dad was just putting red and black paint on his face when she got back to camp. Tony, her younger brother, was putting on his new *regalia*. His outfit, which he had helped his dad work on, was red, decorated with black-tipped felt eagle feathers. It had two *bustles*, and the beadwork was a red, yellow, and blue design.

"Louis better hurry or he won't have time to get dressed and braid his hair," her dad said.

"He stopped to get something to eat, but he'll be here in time," Tina answered, going into the tent. As she got dressed, she remembered how her mother and Aunt Sue had helped her work on her *regalia*. She loved the way the dress felt so silky and cool against her skin. The flowers on the shawl reminded her of wildflowers in the meadow.

10

Tina reached into her bag for her moccasins. She
noticed a little hole starting at the toe of one of them.
She made a face.

"Whatever is the matter, Tina?" her mother asked.

"My moccasins are too small and one of them has a
hole in the toe."

"Fifteen minutes to *Grand Entry*! Fifteen minutes,
dancers!" announced the *emcee*.

Tina felt bad. She knew the judges scored people
not only on their dancing, but on their whole *regalia*.

"We have to get in line for *Grand Entry*," Tina's dad
said. The Howowswee family began to head for the
arena. Just then Tina heard her name being called.
She turned around to see Aunt Sue standing by their
tent. Aunt Sue had a package in her hand.

"Come here quickly, Tina," her aunt said.

Tina started back toward Aunt Sue, but she stopped in her tracks when she saw what her aunt had in her hands. She had made Tina the most beautiful pair of hightop moccasins, with floral beadwork that matched her shawl!

It took Tina no time to get her old moccasins off and the new ones on.

Tina always loved *Grand Entry* and the opening ceremony at the *Powwow*. Today she felt proud to be dancing for the first time with people from all over—Mashpee *Wampanoag, Narragansett, Lakota, Apache, Micmac, Ojibway, Cherokee,* and many more.

When the opening ceremony was over, the crowd heard "*Intertribal*! Everybody dance!" over the loudspeaker. Announcements were made for the Crow Hop, Sneak Up, and other dances.

14

Finally, it was time for the dance competition. Tina held her breath when the Men's Fancy Dance was called. But she shouldn't have worried about her brother Louis. He won first place—$1,000 that he would add to his college fund.

Finally, it was time for the *Fancy Shawl Dance* competition. Tina gave Joanie a big smile, and then looked down at her new moccasins. It was now or never.

Once the drum started, both girls danced and danced. They held their arms out and their heads up, hoping the judges would score them well. Tina felt comfortable and confident in her new moccasins and danced really high on her toes.

After the song, Tina was surprised that the judges asked her and two other girls to dance again. Joanie passed her as she left the arena and whispered, "Don't worry—you're doing great! Good luck!"

Tina smiled and danced again, forgetting how tired she was.

When the dance was over, Tina and Joanie waited together for the judges' decision.

"Girls' *Fancy Shawl Dance*: Third place goes to Tina Howowswee; Second place goes to Rita Ayala; and First place goes to Paula Stephens." Tina could feel her heart pounding!

"We knew you could do it," her mother said as the whole family crowded around her. Tina beamed with happiness.

She had learned a lot today about carrying on Native traditions and she was very proud!

Glossary

bustle (BUHS-uhl) a circle of feathers (usually eagle, hawk, or turkey) which is worn at the back as part of a man's regalia

emcee (EM-see) a master of ceremonies or announcer

Fancy Shawl Dance (FAN-see SHAHL DANS) a modern, fast-moving dance where women wear shawls representing butterflies emerging from cocoons

Grand Entry (GRAHND EN-tree) the beginning of a Powwow when dancers line up and dance into the arena

Howowswee (HOH-wow-swee) a Wampanoag family name

intertribal (in-tur-TRI-bul) a dance at a Powwow in which all tribes participate

Narragansett, Lokota, Apache, Micmac, Ojibway, Cherokee (NAR-rah-GAHN-set, loh-KOH-tah, ah-PACH-ee, MIK-mak, oh-JIB-WAH, CHAR-oh-KEY) Native American tribes

Penobscot (puh-NOB-scaht) a nation of Native American people from Maine

Powwow (POW-wow) a gathering of Native American people where there is dancing, socializing, and the selling of Native crafts and food

regalia (ri-GAYL-yuh) special clothing worn by Native American people at celebrations

Wampanoag (wahm-pah-NOH-og) a nation of Native American people from southeastern Massachusetts

About the Author

Linda Coombs is a member of the Wampanoag tribe of Gay Head, Massachusetts. As the Native American Developer at The Children's Museum, Boston, she has helped to organize many Powwows. In addition, she works in the Wampanoag Indian Program at Plimouth Plantation in Plymouth, Massachusetts. An artist, Ms. Coombs specializes in beadwork and traditional Wampanoag weaving.

About the Illustrator

Carson Waterman was born on the Cattaraugus Indian Reservation of the Seneca Nation of Indians. He is a member of the Snipe Clan of the Seneca Nation and studied at the Cooper School of Art in Cleveland, Ohio. A former instructor at the Cleveland Museum of Art, and exhibit designer, illustrator, and artist at the Seneca-Iroquois National Museum in Salamanca, New York, Mr. Waterman's art has been exhibited throughout the northeastern United States.

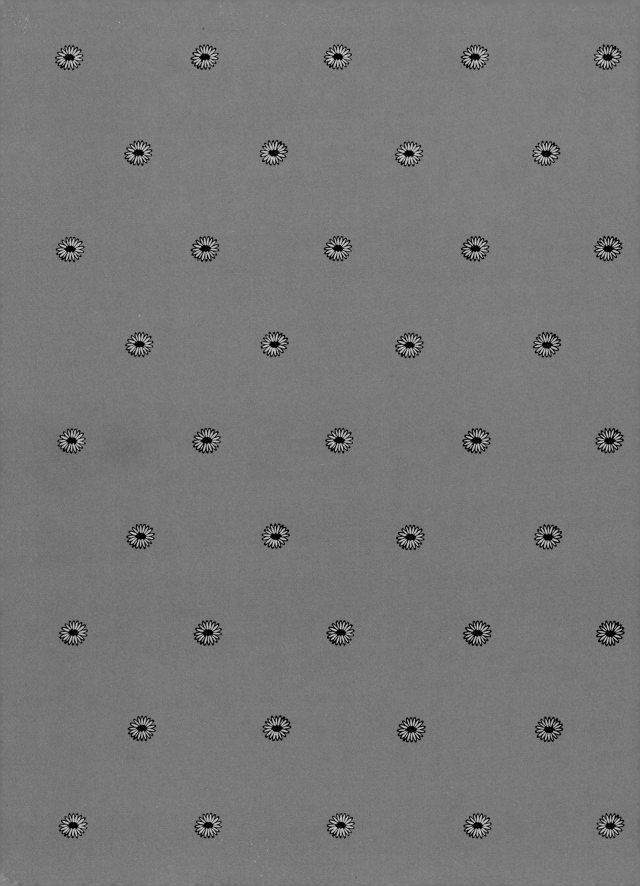